USBORNE FIRST READING

The King's Pudding

Retold by Mairi Mackinnon
Illustrated by Nathalie Ragondet

USBORNE FIRST READING

Danny the Dragon

Russell Punter
Illustrated by Peter Cottrill

The Boy Who Cried Wolf

Retold by Mairi Mackinnon

Illustrated by Mike and Carl Gordon

USBORNE FIRST READING

The Gingerbread Man

retold by Mairi Mackinnon
Illustrated by Elena Temporin

USBORNE FIRST READING

Tom Thumb

Retold by Katie Daynes
Illustrated by Wesley Robins

An Aesop's Fable

The Lion and the Mouse

Retold by Susanna Davidson
Illustrated by John Joven

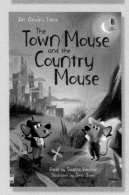

An Aesop's Fable

The Town Mouse and the Country Mouse

Retold by Susanna Davidson
Illustrated by John Joven

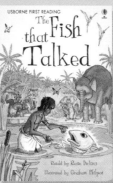

USBORNE FIRST READING

The Fish that Talked

Retold by Rosie Dickins
Illustrated by Graham Philpot

USBORNE FIRST READING

The Magic Porridge Pot

Based on the story by The Brothers Grimm
Illustrated by Mike and Carl Gordon

The Fox and the Stork

Retold by Susanna Davidson
Illustrated by John Joven

Reading consultant: Alison Kelly

Fox loved to play tricks
on friends. Fox played
tricks on Badger.

Fox played tricks on Owl.

Fox played tricks on Bat!

"First, I need to write
Stork a letter," said Fox.

Stork was very excited
to get Fox's letter.

Dear Stork,

Please come to my house for supper at 6 o'clock.

No need to bring anything.

From Fox

Stork spent all day
getting ready.

At half past five, it started to rain. The wind howled.

But Stork didn't want to
let Fox down.

15

Stork arrived, looking very soggy. "Come in, come in," said Fox.

"I've made spicy stew!"

"You must be so hungry," said Fox.

"Oh I am, I am,"
said Stork.

Fox put the stew into
wide, shallow bowls.

"It's my best stew yet,"
said Fox.

Stork tried to eat
the stew...

...but it was IMPOSSIBLE!

Stork looked up to see
Fox laughing.

"You tricked me!" said Stork. "You're supposed to be my friend."

Stork strutted home through the rain.

Stork spent *all night*
thinking up a cunning
plan.

The next morning, Stork
sat down to write a letter.

Fox grinned when the invitation arrived.

"Stork is such a good cook.
I can't wait!"

Fox didn't eat anything
all morning.

At last, it was lunchtime. Fox hurried to Stork's house.

"Hello Stork," said Fox.

"Please, sit down," said Stork.

"I've made you a fish soup."

Oh! I love fish soup!

Stork poured the soup
into tall jars.

"It's delicious!" said Stork.
"My best yet!"

Fox tried EVERYTHING
to drink the soup...

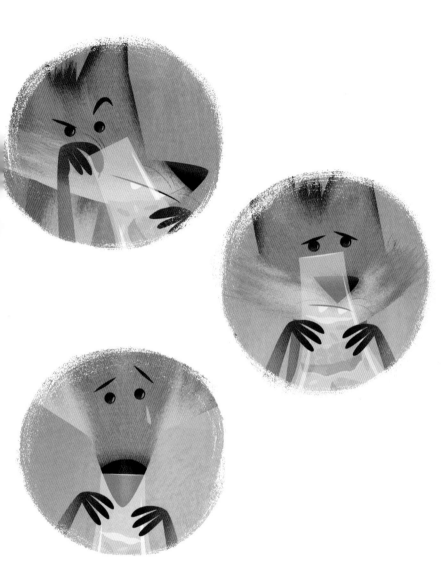

...but it was IMPOSSIBLE!

"You tricked me!"
said Fox.

"I did trick you," said
Stork, with a smile.

"And now you know what it feels like," said Stork.

"It's horrible when someone plays a trick on you," said Stork.

It is.

The next day, Fox said sorry to Badger...

Owl...

and Bat.

Last of all, Fox said
thank you to Stork.

I'll never play
tricks on my
friends again.

About the story

Aesop's Fables are from Ancient Greece. They always have a moral, or a lesson, at the end. The moral of this story is: "Treat others as you'd like to be treated yourself."

Designed by Vickie Robinson
Series designer: Russell Punter
Series editor: Lesley Sims

First published in 2020 by Usborne Publishing Ltd.,
Usborne House, 83-85 Saffron Hill, London EC1N 8RT, England.
usborne.com Copyright © 2020 Usborne Publishing Ltd.